CHICKADEE
CRIMINAL MASTERMIND

For Danny, Jacob and Autumn, with love — M.S.

To my dear friend and my favorite criminal mastermind, Tania Leleka — E.E.

ACKNOWLEDGMENTS

Many thanks to Lisa Cinar and my classmates in the 2017 Illustration for Picture Books class at Emily Carr University of Art + Design: without you *Chickadee: Criminal Mastermind* would never have hatched!

I am grateful to Ildiko Szabo, Collections Curator, UBC Beaty Biodiversity Museum; Mya Thompson, Co-Director for Engagement in Science and Nature, Cornell Lab of Ornithology; and Sarah Wagner, PhD, who kindly checked for any cracks in the manuscript and back matter. Any errors are my own, of course. — M.S.

Text © 2022 Monica Silvie
Illustrations © 2022 Elina Ellis

Published in Canada and the U.S. by Kids Can Press Ltd.
25 Dockside Drive, Toronto, ON M5A 0B5

Kids Can Press is a Corus Entertainment Inc. company

www.kidscanpress.com

The artwork in this book was rendered digitally.
The text is set in Avenir.

Edited by Yasemin Uçar and Kathleen Keenan
Designed by Andrew Dupuis

Printed and bound in Buji, Shenzhen, China, in 10/2021 by WKT Company

CM 22 0 9 8 7 6 5 4 3 2 1

LIBRARY AND ARCHIVES CANADA CATALOGUING IN PUBLICATION

Title: Chickadee : criminal mastermind / Monica Silvie, Elina Ellis.
Names: Silvie, Monica, author. | Ellis, Elina, illustrator.
Description: Written by Monica Silvie and illustrated by Elina Ellis.
Identifiers: Canadiana 20210197854 | ISBN 9781525303388 (hardcover)
Classification: LCC PS8637.I363 C45 2022 | DDC jC813/.6 — dc23

Kids Can Press gratefully acknowledges that the land on which our office is located is the traditional territory of many nations, including the Mississaugas of the Credit, the Anishnabeg, the Chippewa, the Haudenosaunee and the Wendat peoples, and is now home to many diverse First Nations, Inuit and Métis peoples.

We thank the Government of Ontario, through Ontario Creates; the Ontario Arts Council; the Canada Council for the Arts; and the Government of Canada for supporting our publishing activity.

CHICKADEE
CRIMINAL MASTERMIND

Monica Silvie   Elina Ellis

KIDS CAN PRESS

The forest has a criminal. A real rapscallion and all-around bad seed.

And no one knows who I am, because …

I know what you're thinking. "How could you have fallen into a life of crime, Chickadee?"

This is my story.

I grew up in a little hollow at the top of an alder tree, with loving parents who fed me bugs.

And, yes, I was a cute baby.

Awww ...

PEEP

PEEP

PEEP

My parents warned me never to leave the safety of the forest.

I was a good nestling who always listened to their advice.

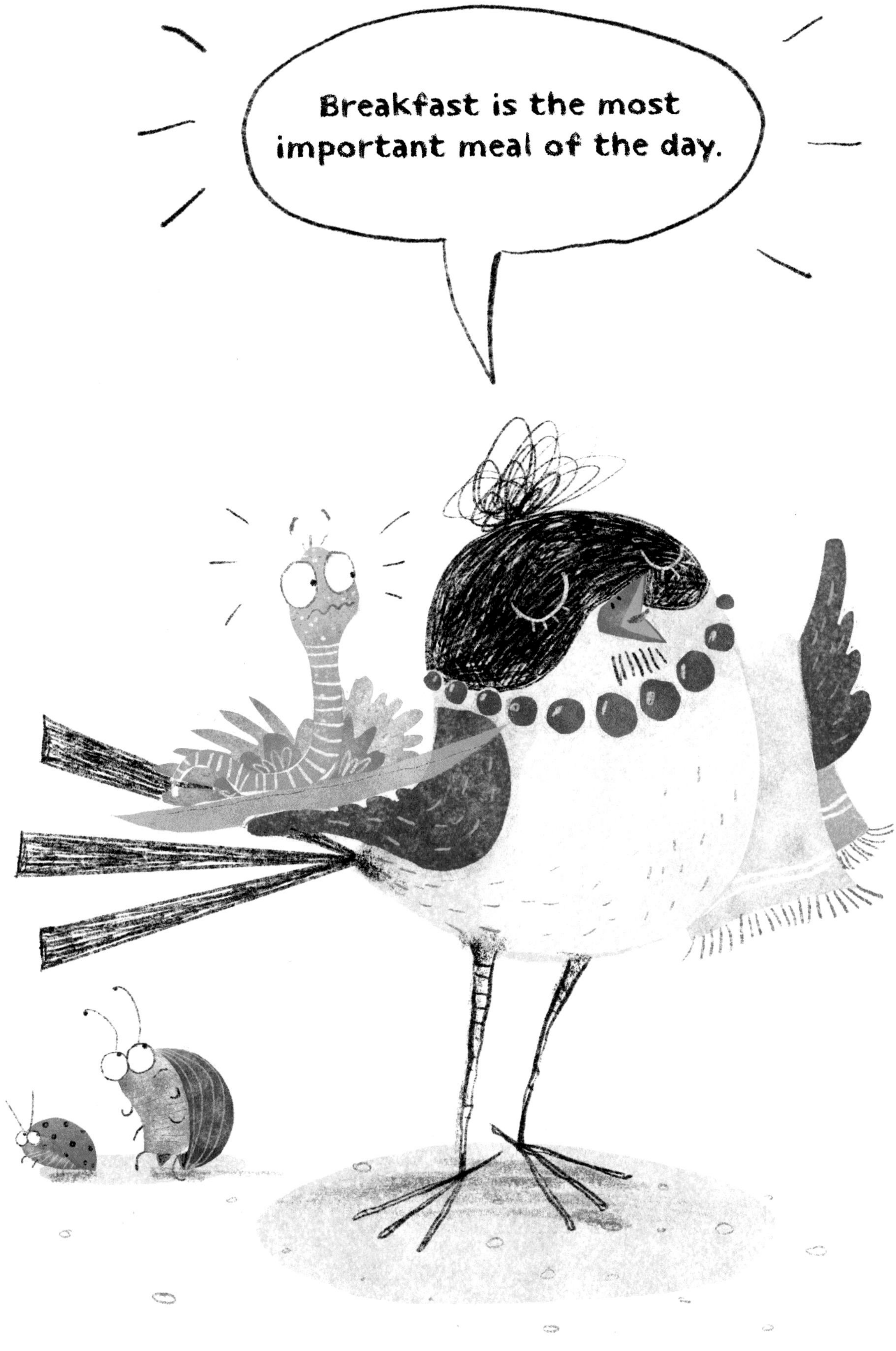
Breakfast is the most important meal of the day.

After a long and happy childhood, I finally left the nest on my sixteenth day.

Call me!

That summer and fall,
I was free as a bird,

learning to catch bugs

and hanging around the forest.

But then came winter.
A shocking thing happened:
cold flakes fell from the sky!
A lot of them!

It became way harder to find
food in the forest.

One snowy morning, on my rounds, I spotted something strange near one of the houses.

Wait, wasn't there something I was supposed to remember about houses?

Hmm ... anyway, I checked it out.

It was a vault of gold.
And I stole from it.

I know what you'll ask me next. "How do you do it, Chickadee? How does a criminal mastermind like you steal gold from a vault?"

Let me demonstrate.

First, I scout the area, checking out my target from every angle.

Then, I swoop in for the prize
and make my escape.

One more successful snatch!
I am the King of Thieves.

I have many secret hiding places in the forest where I keep my stolen treasures. Hundreds, really. But don't worry — I can remember every one.

Between these twigs.

Here, in a crack.

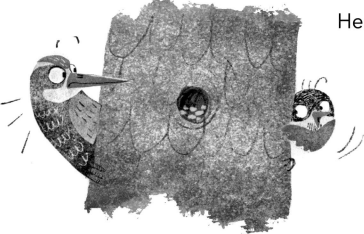

Here, in a woodpecker's hole.

Under this leaf.

Under this branch.

In my secret lair.

In this crevice.

In a hole.

Under the bark.

Here.

You might think that life as a masked villain is exciting — glamorous, even.

Look out, little bird, hawk on the wing!

DEE DEE

CHICKA DEE DEE DEE

Mama!

Hmph. Foiled again!

Thank you, mysterious stranger!

But really, it's just …

… lonely.

I know what you're wondering. "How do you get away with it? How do you avoid justice, Chickadee?"

Let me show you again, this time in slow motion.

I fly up to the vault and —

Ack! I've been spotted!

wait — cute?

I'm not cute!
I'm a rapscallion!
An all-around bad seed!

I consult my underwing dictionary.

Well, there's only one thing to do.

And, so, it turns out I'm not a criminal after all.
I'm not a rapscallion. I'm not even a bad seed.

I'm just a little bird
being a bird.

But maybe I'll finally make a friend!

FACTS ABOUT THE MARVELOUS BLACK-CAPPED CHICKADEE

The species of chickadee featured in this book is a black-capped chickadee. Black-capped chickadees live year-round in much of Canada and the northern half of the United States.

1. BLACK-CAPPED CHICKADEES ARE TOUGH.

Freezing temperatures? No worries! Chickadees just puff up their feathers. This helps them trap air that keeps them warm. In really cold weather, a chickadee can even lower its body temperature to conserve its energy. Some chickadees can survive winter in Alaska, where they encounter temperatures of -50°C (-58°F) and only three and a half hours of daylight.

2. BLACK-CAPPED CHICKADEES HAVE INTERESTING TASTES ...

Favorite foods

Bugs ...

seeds and berries ...

and fat from dead animals!

3. BLACK-CAPPED CHICKADEES HAVE SURPRISING BRAINS.

In the fall, chickadees begin hiding food in multiple places (called "caching"). They can remember hundreds of caches. How do they do it? The number of brain cells in their hippocampus (the area of the brain responsible for spatial memory) increases in winter. That number shrinks down again in summer, as shown in this scientific diagram:

4. BLACK-CAPPED CHICKADEES ARE EXCELLENT COMMUNICATORS.

Chickadees are named for their call, which you may have heard. It often sounds like this: "Chick-a-dee-dee-dee." Chickadees make these calls to communicate information to their flock (a group of birds).

There's a lot going on in a chickadee call, and they don't all sound the same. With our insensitive human ears, we can't hear many differences between calls. But there is one type of call that we can easily pick out. To warn their flock of danger, chickadees often add on many extra DEES. More DEES mean greater danger. A chickadee warning of extreme danger could sound like this to our human ears: "Chick-a-dee-dee-dee-dee-dee-dee-dee-dee-dee-dee!"

To a bird's ears, tiny differences in a chickadee call could give more information, like:
Come here, I found food!
Everybody, freeze! Pygmy owl on this branch!
All clear! Danger's gone!
Hawk on the wing, look out!

In winter, chickadees join mixed flocks made up of birds from different species. All the birds in the flock, and even birds that are not chickadees, seem to understand different chickadee calls.

Chickadees have many other sounds, too. "Fee-bee-ee" (sounds like "Cheese bur-ger" or "Hey sweetie!" with one high note and two lower notes) is the song male chickadees sing, beginning in January, to attract a mate and to warn off other males.

Sometimes females use this song, too, with other meanings. (Maybe they're saying: "What a beautiful day!")

SELECT SOURCES

BOOKS

Erickson, Laura, and Marie Read. *Into the Nest: Intimate Views of the Courting, Parenting, and Family Lives of Familiar Birds*. North Adams, MA: Storey Publishing, 2015.

Harrap, Simon, and David Quinn. *Chickadees, Tits, Nuthatches & Treecreepers*. Princeton, NJ: Princeton University Press, 1995.

Haupt, Lyanda Lynn. *The Urban Bestiary: Encountering the Everyday Wild*. New York: Little, Brown and Company, 2013.

Heinrich, Bernd. *One Wild Bird at a Time: Portraits of Individual Lives*. Boston: Houghton Mifflin Harcourt, 2016.

Thompson III, Bill. *Bird Homes and Habitats*. Boston: Houghton Mifflin Harcourt, 2013.

WEBSITES

https://www.allaboutbirds.org/guide/Black-capped_Chickadee

https://www.npr.org/sections/krulwich/2013/12/23/256576296/what-chickadees-have-that-i-want-badly

FURTHER READING

Eriksson, Ann. *Bird's-Eye View: Keeping Wild Birds in Flight*. Victoria, BC: Orca Book Publishers, 2020.

Hickman, Pamela, and Carolyn Gavin. *Nature All Around: Birds*. Toronto: Kids Can Press, 2020.

Oseid, Kelsey. *Nests, Eggs, Birds: An Illustrated Aviary*. Berkeley, CA: Ten Speed Press, 2020.